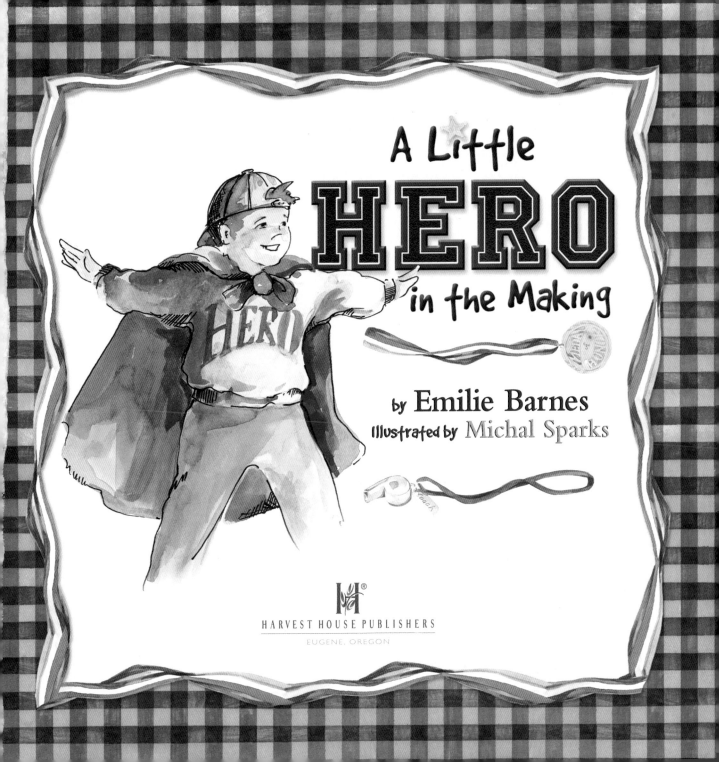

A Little HERO in the Making

by Emilie Barnes

Illustrated by Michal Sparks

HARVEST HOUSE PUBLISHERS

EUGENE, OREGON

A LITTLE HERO IN THE MAKING

Emilie Barnes with Janna Walkup

Copyright © 2007 Emilie Barnes
Published by Harvest House Publishers
Eugene, OR 97402
ISBN-13: 978-0-7369-1978-4
ISBN-10: 0-7369-1978-3

Design and Production: Garborg Design Works, Minneapolis, Minnesota

Printed in China

07 08 09 10 11 / LP / 10 9 8 7 6 5 4 3

CONTENTS

BE A HERO—MASTER

YOUR MANNERS!

Do you ever imagine yourself a hero? Maybe you tie on a bright red cape and do amazing things—like fly around the world! Or maybe you stick closer to earth and drive a racing red fire truck or score the winning point at the very last second!

Heroes do incredible things, and they can do them because they work hard and have good, brave hearts. For instance, your doctor *listens* to you to figure out how to help you feel better. Your teacher or coach *helps* you and other children learn new games and skills. And your dad *cares* about you enough to teach you how to throw a ball or tie your shoes.

Listening and *sharing* and *caring* are all things that heroes do—and you can do these things, too!

So are you ready to become a real-world hero? Got your cape tied on? Ready to become a little hero "in the making"? Great! Let's get ready to fly... and master those manners!

I CAN BE A HERO BY...
Helping at Home

It's time to open your eyes and see where our journey to becoming a hero has taken us. Hey! You recognize this place, don't you? It's your very own home!

Home is the best place to begin mastering your manners. With your family and all of your favorite toys and books—and maybe even a cuddly pet—you'll love starting your hero training here!

Let's start by learning how to say the strongest words in the world. Strongest *words*?! Yes! Get ready—here they come...

Please.
Thank you.
Excuse me.
I'm sorry.

These are words that save the world. They show others that you care and that you're willing to do the right thing. That's what heroes do!

With your family, you can practice doing all the things that heroes do. You can be kind. You can be helpful. You can be giving. You can be obedient.

KIND

And did you know that heroes even follow rules? You bet they do! Every hero follows something called the Golden Rule:

Do unto others as you would have them do unto you.

This just means that you can treat people in the way that *you* would like to be treated. Do you like to get help making your bed or picking up your toys? Sure! Then you can *help* others. Do you like getting gifts? Of course! Then you can *give* to others. Do you like things to be fair? Yes! Then you can *play fair* with others.

HONEST

HELPFUL

When you're at home, you can start your hero training by listening to your parents and doing what they ask. Put your things away. Come when you're called. Always tell the truth. Be kind to your brothers and sisters and pets.

You can be a hero — by helping out at home!

YOU CAN BE AN EVERYDAY HERO

I CAN BE A HERO BY...
Being a Great Playmate

Hey! Now we're flying! We're headed away from home and whoosh—*bump!* Here we are at your favorite playground. Look!

There's that fast slide that you love! And the swing where you fly high! But wait a second... there's already a line for both of those. I guess the first thing we need to talk about is *sharing*.

10

Heroes *share*
with others—they
give them their time,
their toys, and their talents.
They know that waiting
patiently and taking turns are
noble acts. Not everyone
can do those things, but
heroes can!

11

HONEST

Heroes follow the rules. They smile when they win, and they can laugh when they lose. They always play fair and never cheat. When someone gets hurt, they are there to say, "Are you all right? Are you okay?"

So you can wait patiently for your turn. You can share your blocks and cars with a pal. You can even be a great playmate for pets by being kind to them and helping care for them!

Did you know that little acts of kindness—like saying "You can go first" or giving someone a nice smile—are just as important as big deeds of bravery? Everything adds up, and you can save someone's day by being kind!

You can be a hero—by being a great playmate!

I CAN BE A HERO BY...
Exploring My World

Here! Take this flashlight! And you might need this map and compass. Oh, and let's switch on these walkie-talkies. It's time to explore!

Sure, a hero knows how to save the world. But first, a hero needs to know how to act in his world. So let's get going!

When you visit your grandparents' house or go to the library or eat out at a restaurant, you're exploring. You're discovering how to talk and act in a new place. What an adventure!

HELLO
How are you?

Sometimes when you're out exploring your world, you might meet someone who looks or acts a little different. But inside, they are just the same as you. They deserve a hero's friendship, too!

The best thing to do when you meet anyone new is to smile at them and say "hello." You can shake their hand—that's a *very* grown-up thing to do. Right now, it's best to meet new people when you're with your parents or another adult that you know very well. That way, you can stay safe *and* learn what to do and say. When you're ready to leave, be sure to say a friendly "goodbye."

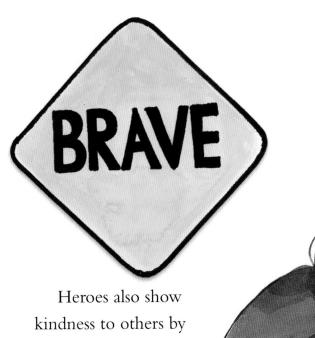

Heroes also show kindness to others by calling them what they would like to be called—Mr. Lawnmower or Mrs. Snapdragon or Dr. Sniffle. That shows kindness and respect—and it's very brave of you.

You can be a hero—by exploring your world!

YOU CAN BE AN EVERYDAY HERO

Wow! I bet that person would like to sit down— but there are no more chairs! I know what to do...

Oh thanks! — Hey, you're a real little hero!

Sometimes you just need to give a hero hug!

4

I CAN BE A HERO BY...
Taking Care of Myself

Here we go again, flying along... looking for our next spot to land. Hey! What's that bright, shiny thing over there? Let's fly a little closer. It looks like a mirror! What does *that* have to do with being a hero? Oh, look—there *you* are in the reflection! You have your hero cape on, and you certainly look brave. But...hmm...is that lettuce in your teeth? And when was the last time you washed your cape? Looks like we need to take care of a few things first.

Heroes take care of other people—and animals—in need, but they also take care of someone else who's very important. *Themselves!*

Combed hair and clean clothes go very well with a bright red hero cape. So do brushed and flossed teeth and a big smile. The quicker you catch on to washing and dressing yourself, the quicker you can get on with your fun and playtime. So be sure to practice taking care of yourself every day! Of course, it's okay to wear clothes that are old or dirty when you play. But you should wear something clean to a birthday party or church.

It's hard to save the world when you're sick. Every hero gets the sneezes and sniffles from time to time, but there are some things you can do all by yourself to keep from getting sick. Be sure to wash your hands a lot—especially after going to the bathroom and before you eat. To help keep others safe and healthy, remember to blow your nose into a tissue and cover your mouth when you cough. Thanks for helping!

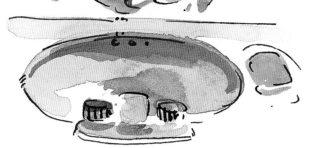

You can be a hero—by taking care of yourself!

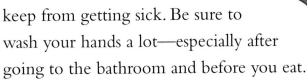

I CAN BE A HERO BY...
Eating Like a Champion!

Whoa! Slow down! You're flying too fast! Aaaahhhh—oops! Where on earth did you land? And what's that on your hero cape? Looks like vegetable soup. And peanut butter and jelly in your hair. I guess our next stop is the lunch table!

STRONG

BRAVE

To be a hero, you need to grow big and strong. And you can do that by eating healthy foods— fruits and vegetables, proteins, and vitamins. Even if you don't think you will like something, be brave! Spinach or almond butter just might end up being one of your favorite foods—well, or maybe just not so bad after all. If something truly tastes awful—or if you're allergic to it—a simple "No, thank you" will do.

You can also be a hero by mastering your table manners—the way you eat and the things you say and do during breakfast, lunch, and dinner. It's always a good idea asking to help get the food ready or set the table. And be

sure to wash your hands and come right away when you're called. Sit up straight in your chair, keep your mouth closed when chewing your food, and say "Excuse me" or "I'm sorry" if you accidentally spill something or do something you shouldn't have.

I'm sorry

Excuse me

May I be excused?

Thank you

When your food is in your tummy and you're ready to run and play, it's a good idea to ask "May I please be excused?" before you run off. Say thank you to the cook for the tasty meal, and then you're on your way!

You can be a hero — by eating like a champion!

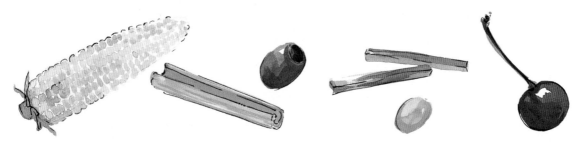

6

I CAN BE A HERO BY...
Having a Brave Heart

Wow! This has been some journey! You've learned about all there is to learn about being a real hero in your world. The adventure is almost over, but before you go, we have just one more thing to discover.

BRAVE

28

While the heroes we wish to be might have strong arms or great ideas or amazing powers, one thing they all have is a brave heart. And a brave heart starts inside you with kindness. In fact, two small words hold the key to kindness. These are magic words:

Thank you.

thank you !

These magic words make everyone feel good—both the person being thanked *and* the person saying thank you! And even though you might not always be able to use your superpowers, you can *always* use these magic words. They always work, too!

Just about any time is a good time to use the magic "thank you" words. Pull them out of your cape whenever anyone says something nice about you, helps you, gives you a present, or invites you over for playtime or to a party.

Thanks!

KIND

You can say the words in person,
on the telephone, with a hug, or even
draw them into a picture. No matter
how you do it, give me a high-five!
You'll always be a hero!

You can be a hero—
by having a brave heart!